Lost and Found

PENGUIN WORKSHOP
Penguin Young Readers Group
An Imprint of Penguin Random House LLC

Text copyright © 2019 by Erica S. Perl. Illustrations copyright © 2019 by Penguin Random House LLC. All rights reserved. Published by Penguin Workshop, an imprint of Penguin Random House LLC, 345 Hudson Street, New York, New York 10014. PENGUIN and PENGUIN WORKSHOP are trademarks of Penguin Books Ltd, and the W colophon is a registered trademark of Penguin Random House LLC. Manufactured in China.

Library of Congress Cataloging-in-Publication Data is available.

ISBN 9781524790424 (paperback)   10 9 8 7 6 5 4 3 2 1
ISBN 9781524790431 (library binding)   10 9 8 7 6 5 4 3 2 1

Arnold and Louise

Lost and Found

by Erica S. Perl

illustrated by Chris Chatterton

Penguin Workshop

An Imprint of Penguin Random House

To Mike. Without you, I'd be lost—ESP

Chapter One

Arnold collected things.

Rocks. Pinecones. Sticks

shaped like letters.

They were his treasures.

Louise did not collect things.

"I only need the sun in the sky," she explained.

But it wasn't just that Louise didn't collect things.

Louise also lost things.

Usually, Arnold's things.

One day, Arnold found the best treasure ever.

It was shiny and blueish greenish and—

"Can I see it? Can I have it?" asked Louise.

Arnold shook his head.

"I need it for my Blue Things collection," he told her.

"It's more green than blue," she said.

"Then for my Green Things collection."

"Is this because I lost your favorite acorn cap?" Louise asked.

"And my second-favorite acorn cap," Arnold reminded her.

"See!" said Louise. "You're still mad!"

"Louise, you lose everything," said Arnold.

"I don't! I won't," said

5

Louise. "I'll just borrow it until tomorrow. Pleeeeeease?"

Arnold considered.

Louise did her best to look trustworthy.

Finally, Arnold nodded.

With a happy squeal, Louise ran off with the treasure.

"You won't be sorry!" she called.

Arnold hoped she was right.

Chapter Two

The next morning, Arnold went to find Louise.

But she wasn't
home.

Arnold sat
down to wait.
He closed
his eyes.

Hop!
Hop!
Bop!

11

"Ow!" said Arnold, grabbing his nose.

"Now you have to find me!" yelled Louise, darting into the bushes.

12

"I just came to get my treasure," said Arnold.

"Relax, Arnold," said Louise, peeking out. "Your treasure is safe. So now we can play Hop-Hop-Bop!"

Arnold raised one eyebrow.

"Hop-Hop-Bop?" he asked.

"Yes!" said Louise. "It's like hide-and-seek. But with hopping. *And* bopping!"

"Can I at least have my treasure back first?" asked Arnold.

"Your treasure is hidden," said Louise.

"Hidden?"

"Yes! That's how Hop-Hop-Bop works."

"But, Louise—" said Arnold.

"Just give it a try," said Louise. "Start looking and I'll say if you're hot or cold. Ready? Go!"

Arnold sighed. He walked
toward the creek.

"You're cold, Arnold. Hop!"
said Louise.

Arnold turned and started to walk toward a big tree.

"No, really. You have to hop," explained Louise.

Arnold hopped toward the tree.

"Brrr . . . getting colder. Hop-Hop!" said Louise.

Arnold hopped in the other direction.

"You're an icicle!" Louise giggled. "Hop-Hop—!"

"STOP!" shouted Arnold.

"Louise, I have looked—and

hopped—in EVERY direction."

"Every direction but one,"

said Louise.

19

Just then Arnold heard

tweet, tweet, tweet.

He looked up.

"You're getting warmer,"

said Louise.

Chapter Three

"You gave my treasure

away?" asked Arnold.

"Not exactly," said Louise.

"So, you lost it?"

"Of course not!"

"Then what happened to my treasure?!"

"Excuse me," said a voice. "Oh good, it is you. Do you want to see how it looks?"

Louise nodded.

She was up the tree in a flash.

"Arnold, you have to come see this," called Louise.

Arnold squinted up at her.

He wanted to stop playing the game.

But he also wondered what Louise wanted to show him.

Arnold took a deep breath and started to climb.

26

He came upon a nest of baby birds and their mother. "What are you?" asked the baby birds.

"I'm a bear," said Arnold.

"Ooooo!" The baby birds' eyes opened wide.

"Are you going to eat us?" peeped the tiniest one.

"Of course he's not!" said their mother. "He's here to see our new mirror. I'm trying to figure out if this is the right spot for it."

"Actually, I just—" Arnold

28

started to say, but then he

saw it.

His treasure.

There it was, so close he

could touch it.

And it was as beautiful as

he remembered.

Suddenly, a surprising

feeling came over him as

he watched the baby birds

dance.

"Mir-ror! Mir-ror!" they sang

happily.

"It's . . . perfect," said

Arnold, "right where it is."

Chapter Four

On the ground again,

Arnold thanked Louise.

"Today you gave me a

treasure I can keep forever,"

he said.

Louise looked confused. "Can I see it?" she asked.

Arnold shook his head. "You can't *see* it because it's a feeling," he explained. "It's a good feeling, and it's more important than a thing."

"Hey, maybe you can start a feelings collection," suggested Louise.

Arnold smiled. "Maybe I will."

"Thanks for having us!"

Louise called up to the nest.

"Thank *you*, dear," the mother bird replied. She laughed. "That mirror was good and stuck in the mud down by the creek. If you hadn't come along and helped me pull it out, I would have had to leave it."

Arnold looked at Louise.

"In the mud? By the creek? So you *did* lose my treasure."

"I did not," said Louise. "She found it. I just said she could have it."

"She only found it because you lost it!"

"Why are you so mad?"
asked Louise. "You said you
had a good feeling.

And you said feelings are more important than things."

"My good feeling is gone!" said Arnold. "You must have lost that, too!"

Then he walked away, fast.

"Arnold, wait up. I found a really cool rock for you," said Louise.

Arnold did not wait up.

"Arnold, stop! I found pinecones. Your favorite kind, lots of them."

Arnold did not stop.

"Arnold, I found a stick shaped like the letter *A*! Come look," said Louise.

Arnold did not come look.

"FINE. I LOSE THINGS!" yelled

Louise. "I don't mean to, but I

do."

"Please, Arnold," she added. "I don't want to lose my best friend."

Chapter Five

Arnold turned

around.

He walked back over.

Louise held out the *A* stick.

"I won't even ask to borrow

it!" she said happily.

Arnold examined the stick.

He had to admit, it was perfect for his collection.

"It's a really nice stick," said Louise. "I mean, for your collection. Though, if you know someone who doesn't have a stick collection and wants to start one . . ."

Arnold looked down at the stick.

He looked at Louise.

There were a million sticks in the forest.

But there was only one Louise.

Just then, Arnold realized that he still had the good feeling.

Apparently, it was a treasure even Louise couldn't lose.

"You can keep it, if you want," said Arnold.

"Really?" said Louise.

Arnold nodded.

They walked on together, Louise holding the stick tightly.

"I thought you just needed the sun in the sky," said Arnold.

"Yes," said Louise. "And this stick."

"Even if you lose the stick," said Arnold, "you are never going to lose me."

"Promise?" asked Louise.

Arnold answered by gently

bopping her nose.

Louise smiled. "No bopping

without hopping!" she said.

"Wait a minute, I'll hide."

She hopped off, her stick held high.

"I wasn't really worried," Louise called. "We're best friends, after all."

"We are," agreed Arnold.

"Besides," added Louise,

"you're much too big to lose."